Donkey—donkey

by Roger Duvoisin

PARENTS' MAGAZINE PRESS · NEW YORK

Donkey-donkey was a nice little donkey.
His ears were just long enough.
His belly was white and round as a ball.

Donkey-donkey had many very dear
friends. Here are some of them:

Here are some others:

Pit and Pat, the horses, and Hector,
the dog, also were his friends.

Donkey-donkey's master was the
kindest man in the village.

Donkey-donkey loved thistles
for his dinner, and there were
a lot of them near the little
stream across the meadow.

Yet, in spite of all that, Donkey-donkey
was not happy. One day he was
drinking with Pat at the stream.

He saw Pat's head and
his own in the water.

He thought Pat was so beautiful
with his small ears, and he so ridiculous
with his long ones that he became
very sad and would not eat anymore.

Donkey-donkey at last
went to see Hector.
Hector was very clever.
He knew all sorts of tricks.
He could tell his right paw
from his left paw,
and so on. Surely his
advice would be good.

"You poor donkey,"
said Hector.
"I know what's
wrong with you.
With your ears up
like that, you resemble
a sailboat. Keep your
ears down as I do.

"See how funny I would look
with my ears up!

"That's it, Donkey-donkey,
put them down. Now they look
almost as nice as mine. And Pat will
be jealous because he can't do that."

And Donkey-donkey was happy again.
He went trotting around the farm
like a little colt.

But poor Donkey-donkey.
How his friends laughed
when they saw him!

"Silly donkey," said Fuzzy-fuzzy,
the lamb. "Why do you believe
what Hector says? There is only
one way to wear ears. Look at me!

"Doesn't everyone say I am pretty?

"And look at Phoebe, the goat!

"And look at Fanny, the cow!

"And look at the farmer's brother!

"Do you see how they all put their
ears on the side? So many people
cannot be wrong, Donkey-donkey."

Donkey-donkey was impressed.
He let Fuzzy-fuzzy fix his long ears.
"Now," said the lamb, "you are beautiful.
Wait, let's fetch a mirror!"

Donkey-donkey agreed that he did look
dainty. Naomi, the hen, said the mirror
flattered him. But she had a bad disposition
and of course she *would* say that.

So Donkey-donkey went away again,
happy although somewhat doubtful,
as you can see by his expression.

This is the stable door with a scythe
hanging on a big nail and
Donkey-donkey just about to enter.

He entered as usual. But unfortunate
donkey! The wicked nail met his ear
and pierced it painfully.

Donkey-donkey was sadder than ever.
He cried all night long. It was very
unpleasant for his friends. They could not
sleep. They were quite angry with him.

The next day Donkey-donkey decided
to consult Rosa, the mother pig.
She was not known to be very clever.
She ate and slept so much. But she was
a very honest person. Rosa listened
attentively to Donkey-donkey's grievances.

"Let me think," she said. And she
closed her eyes to think more deeply.

But pigs have slow minds. Donkey-donkey
waited a long time. He counted up to
one hundred, but Rosa was still thinking.
I suspect in fact that she just went to sleep.

At last she opened her eyes and she said,
"Donkey-donkey, I don't know much
about making people look prettier.
But I can give you some practical advice:
The idea of wearing ears up and down
and sideways is all foolishness.
When they are up, the wind and rain
get in them. When they are down, you
can't hear and when they are sideways,
well . . . you know what happens.

"But if you keep them in front, like mine,
then you don't need an umbrella.
You laugh at the sun and at the rain
and you can hear well. Ugh! Ugh!"
And Rosa, who had never spoken so much
in her life, went to sleep.

Donkey-donkey tried it at once.
He thought it really was a very good idea.

Two days later there was a lot of wind
and rain. Pat caught cold and had
the mumps. He had to stay in for a week.
He was much ashamed. Donkey-donkey
did not catch cold. He was delighted,
although he felt sorry for Pat
of course. But . . .

This is to show the inconvenience
of wearing one's ears in front
and of being unable to see the sun
and other things up in the air:

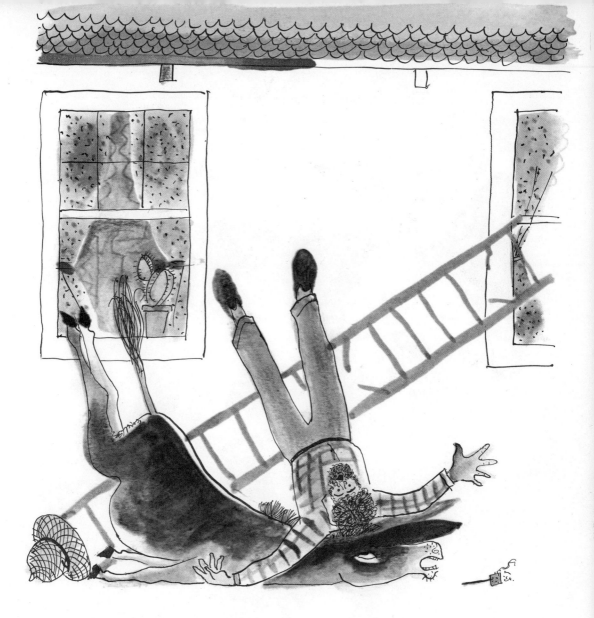

Mr. Jones, the farmer, was painting his house.
His ladder, being too old, broke. Mr. Jones
fell. He fell on Donkey-donkey's head,
and they both fell to the ground. And . . .

... Donkey-donkey was very ill.
The doctor was called in.

He bandaged
his wounds.

He pulled his tongue.

He felt his pulse.

He put him on a scale.
He listened to his
breathing.
And then he gave
him some
bad-tasting medicine
with a spoon.

Donkey-donkey's wounds were soon healed.
But he was still unhappy about his ears.
Everything he tried had failed. As he
was brooding over these sad things,
Daniel, the little sparrow, perched
on the nearby fence.

He said, "Donkey-donkey, silly donkey.
You aren't a dog. You aren't a lamb.
You aren't a pig. You are a donkey.
Keep your ears up as donkeys do.
Twitt! Twitt! Twitt!"
And Daniel flew swiftly away.

Donkey-donkey was astonished.
But he was delighted when a little girl
passing by with her father said,
"Oh! Daddy! See the pretty little donkey.
His ears are so beautiful!"

And from that day Donkey-donkey
kept his ears up. He enjoyed
eating thistles again and he became
the happiest of donkeys.

. . . and this story is finished.

ROGER DUVOISIN was born in Geneva, Switzerland where he graduated from art school and later painted murals, stage designs, posters and illustrations. He also worked in ceramics and at one time was manager of a French pottery plant. He actually came to the United States as a designer for an American textile firm. But, happily, one day he wrote and illustrated a book for his young son, thus beginning a career that was to make him internationally famous as the creator of beautiful picture books for children.

Among the books Mr. Duvoisin has written and illustrated are *The Christmas Whale, The Happy Lion,* the *Petunia* and *Veronica* series and many, many others. In 1948 he was awarded a Caldecott medal for his art work in *White Snow, Bright Snow* by Alvin Tresselt. Mr. Duvoisin now makes his home in Gladstone, New Jersey.